A
ROCK
AND A
HARD
PLACE

SHANE TOWNSEND

Fulton Books, Inc.
Meadville, PA

Published by Fulton Books 2020

ISBN 978-1-64654-282-6 (paperback)
ISBN 978-1-64654-283-3 (digital)

Printed in the United States of America

PROLOGUE

I stood on the second of four steps leading up to the brand-new building at the intersection of University and Lexington in St. Paul, contemplating whether or not I should follow through with my plan of action. It was a very brief contemplation, about one-tenth of a second or so, but in that short span of time, a million thoughts went through my head. Some were questioning my sanity. Most were regarding the consequences of my actions.

University and Lexington is a very busy intersection and very noisy. I heard none of the noise and saw none of the congested traffic. What had my attention as part of my brief thought process was the little devil sitting on my left shoulder. Those of you who have watched *Tom and Jerry* know what I am talking about.

"Come on dog, what are you waiting for?" he whispered slyly in my ear. "It's time to handle this business and get this money!" he said more forcefully.

A little angel then appeared on my right shoulder.

"Are you kidding me?" he asked. "You're messing with them white folk's money, and you know that if they catch you—no, WHEN they catch you—they're gonna bury your yella ass UNDER the jail, and they're gonna throw away the key!"

In rebuttal, the little devil argued, "You done lost your job, you've been deathly ill, your bills are piling up, and your bitch is treating you like some random nigga off the street, talkin' all greasy and shit. This next sixty seconds will solve all of your problems."

That little devil then proceeded to show me a slideshow in my mind of all the pain, misery, suffering, and mistreatment I had suffered over the previous few months. Once that slideshow started, the little angel never stood a chance. Each painful image in my head was a blow to any argument the well-intentioned angel could attempt to make, and in the end, those blows were like a Mike Tyson barrage, beating the little angel down until he crumpled, quieted, and soon just disappeared. All that was left was the little devil urging me on. As I look back on it now, it amazes me how much information flashed through my mind in that one-tenth of a second.

Anyway, I proceeded up the steps and into the building where I went to the counter of an island in the center of the open floor. It was a small building, and it was not far to the windows of the cashiers straight ahead of me. I wrote the following message on the back of a deposit slip: "This is a robbery. Pass over all the loose twenties, fifties, and hundreds. No banded bills and no dye packs, and nobody will get hurt."

After the briefest of pauses, the teller opened her drawer and began handing me the loose bills in the denominations that I had requested, acting as though it were a regular transaction. This is what she had been trained to do. When she finished that, she handed me a banded stack of five-dollar bills, the band denoting that it was worth five hundred dollars. Seeing the anomaly instantly, not as dumb as she must have thought I was, I gave her a quick mean mug, but she remained as cool, calm, and collected as she had been throughout the ordeal. *Slick bitch*, I thought as I tossed the dye pack back across the counter to her. I later learned that my suspicions had been correct regarding the dye pack.

"Nice try," I spoke for the first and only time since I had entered the bank.

Paying her no more mind, I finished stuffing my pockets with cash then hastily made my way out of the bank. I crossed the street once I had made it across the bank parking lot then ran half a block to the nearest alley where I took a right. I then began to remove my top layer of clothes and tossed them into a nearby garbage can. I also removed my ball cap that I had on and my glasses. I wasn't too worried about being observed because most people in that neighborhood would be at work during that time of day.

I was a totally different person when I exited that alley on Oxford Avenue. I headed south, back to University Avenue, where I joined a group of students from the local alternative school as they gawked at the police cars driving by at a fast pace, sirens blaring. When I spotted a number sixteen bus headed toward downtown St. Paul, and far away from the bank, I hurried across the street, hopped on it, paid my fare, and sat quietly down. I kept feeling the lumps in my pocket as we rode, amazed at the feeling after being so broke for the past couple of months and still not really believing that I had just done what I did. When I got downtown, I went to the nearest cab stand and took a cab the rest of the way home.

Sounds stupid, huh? But who's gonna look for a bank robber on a bus? Plus, this way I didn't have to worry about someone getting a description of my minivan or my license plate number. Think about it.

CHAPTER 1

Not very exciting, huh? That scenario is not what you'd normally imagine when the subject of bank robbery is mentioned. There were no guns, no hostage taking, no big bags full of money, and no *bang-bang*, shoot-'em-up, Bonnie-and-Clyde type of shit. That was by design. My aim was to get in and get out as fast as possible with as little fanfare and attention drawn to myself as possible. Nobody but me and the teller knew what had transpired until I was a reasonable distance from that establishment.

But I had accomplished what I had set out to do. I was leaving with about five stacks for sixty seconds worth of work. Even as I left though, my subconscious mind began looking forward to the next heist, despite the fact that I had told myself before the robbery that it would be a onetime thing. Even though that had not been an action-packed event, it gave me an adrenaline rush that created an instant, unexpected addiction. It was an addiction to rival any heroin or crack addiction.

Thus began the adventure of a lifetime. This type of hustle suited me perfectly because I prefer to do my dirt solo dolo due to the fact that I had been ratted on before. And like the robberies, burglaries, and low-level drug dealings I had done previously, I knew it would be a low risk if I was careful and that many of these low-risk robberies would equal a lot of cash.

On the bus, I had replayed the robbery from beginning to end. Never in my wildest dreams would I have thought that a bank robbery would be so easy. And never had I felt the elation that I had felt after I had successfully pulled off that robbery. The sheer balls that it had taken to continue up those steps and follow through with my intentions amazed me. The act itself caused unbelievable levels of tension, fear, exhilaration, and excitement, and all those feelings combined to become an indescribable sensation that immediately etched itself permanently into every part of me: physical, mental, and spiritual. And yet I continued to tell myself that it would never happen again, but now that I think about it, I know that I never really believed that.

I got caught after fifteen robberies, which is a blessing because I know that if I had been able to continue, I would have escalated the degree of risk at some point or gotten greedy. Just like a heroin addict, my tolerance would have built to the point where I would need more and more to satisfy my craving. Eventually I would have ended up catching a body or being given a life sentence.

CHAPTER 2

You see, I am predisposed to addiction, both genetically and environmentally. This is why the first adrenaline rush that I experienced while robbing a bank made it impossible for me not to continue down that path, especially when things got rough. I have always turned to drugs and alcohol to cover my pain and anger, but since I had ceased doing that, this replacement was totally acceptable to and welcomed by me.

I am of a mixed race, black and white, my mother being of the Caucasian persuasion and my father being one of the many lost black souls that populate this country. My mother only messes with black men, and somewhere along the way, some black man turned her out on coke and urged her into the occasional prostitution endeavor. The coke and prostitution caused her to abandon me more than once, and I ended up in foster homes until she could convince the courts that she had changed and was competent to once again take charge of her child. I wish she would have just left me where I was. I would have been better off.

She continued to do coke occasionally after the last time she was granted custody of me, and she was a daily and frequent partaker of marijuana throughout my childhood all the way up until I left home, with its rampant and violent abuse at the hands of my stepfather. I was thirteen years old then. I decided that I would rather face the streets than continue to suffer the abuse that I had been subjected to. I don't know about the coke these days, but I do know that she is still a pothead.

My father was a frequent visitor and guest of our state's penal institutions. Most of my earliest memories regarding him pertain to visiting him in various prisons throughout the state with my mother. Once they were divorced when I was about four years old, I almost never saw him. If I was lucky, I would see him between incarcerations. I have never discussed with him his addiction issues, but I have heard things over the years. Add that to the fact that my mother was a cokehead, and I can only assume that my father had the same problem. His frequent trips to prison support that assumption. He just cannot stay his ass out of prison, so he must have the affliction to this day.

My predisposition, coupled with the anger I have for my mother for allowing her own seed to be so severely abused and for abandoning me and the anger that I felt toward my father for abandoning me to the abuse of my stepfather and not being the protector, guide, and mentor that I needed, was corrosive mentally and emotionally, and I became the type of person to do what needed to be done without thought to the consequence or how it affected other people. I was psychologically crippled for most of my life, so rather than seek positive solutions to my problems, I did what came naturally to me: I went out and got that paper. I had no compunctions about running up in them people's financial institutions.

CHAPTER 3

But let me back up for a minute so I can explain what drove me to the point where I felt that I had to take such drastic and foolhardy action. I have a long history of bad choices whether they be the decisions to commit various crimes or my choices in women. I have done time for infractions or the law relating to some of them. Usually it was a choice between me enduring the struggle as a square and me taking the easy way out.

I thought that I had left all of that behind me. During my last incarceration, I had supposedly wised up. I realized that that prison shit was tired, and frankly I was sick of the shit. I knew that all the aptitude tests I had taken in prison weren't lying and that I possessed the intelligence and potential needed to be successful in any endeavor that I wanted to pursue if I just put my mind to it. All I had to do was stop dwelling on my past, forgive others their transgressions, stop blaming "the man," and cease my criminal, abusive, misogynistic ways. Not an easy task but definitely doable.

There was a long period of time then that I was doing everything that needed to be done to make me a better person and help me remain free. I was drug- and alcohol-free, and I was attending AA and NA on a regular basis. Thoughts of higher learning had entered my mind. I had my own place and a minivan that I had purchased. I was working a square ass gig and living a square ass life in general. I was enjoying my new life and my freedom immensely.

There were a few random women in my life at that time but nobody special. All of them were women I had been hooking up with before I had gotten locked up. Not one of them broads had maintained contact with me or sent me money while I was gone. You know how it goes. Out of sight, out of mind. So while fucking them was all right, there was no possibility of anything meaningful with any of them. I was looking for a lady whom I could be my new, more respectful, more caring self with, but none of them fit the bill.

Then I met Brandy.

CHAPTER 4

I was working at the local charity fundraising office, seeking donations for the local needy causes, when in walked Miss Brandy's fine ass. I remember how the sight of her caused me to pause in the middle of my pitch and almost lost a sale.

"Mr. Anderson," I was saying to the gentleman on the phone, "your generosity will go toward helping to find a cure for the many illnesses and afflictions being suffered by those angelic children at the Minneapolis Children's Hospital. As a token of our appreciation, we are going to send you…"

I stopped suddenly, stuck on stupid and unable to finish my sentence because I was mesmerized by the lips and hips on the beautiful redbone chick who had appeared before me suddenly and who had momentarily captured my full attention. I vaguely heard Mr. Anderson in the background asking if I was still there.

When I came out of my trance, I said to Mr. Anderson, "I apologize, Mr. Anderson. I was distracted by the coffee I just spilled. Clumsy me. As I was saying, as a token of our appreciation, we are going to send you a pair of tickets to the upcoming Kenny Chesney concert. Thank you so very much for your generous contribution. You are doing a great thing here. If you will just hold for a second, I will pass you on to my supervisor, Jake, who will verify your pledge. Here's Jake, and thanks again."

The whole time I was making my pitch, my eyes were roaming conspicuously and unabashedly over the generous curves, thighs, breasts, and the sexy ass lips of the angel who had miraculously appeared in my life like the answer to all my prayers. This all occurred back in the days before political correctness made it a fireable offense to even compliment a woman on her outfit or her new hairstyle. She was obviously a new hire, and Terrance, one of the office managers, was showing her around the office and explaining her new job to her. He was flirting with her and showing off because he had a little position, but she seemed to pay his flirting no mind. She wasn't rude, though, and as she responded to him, she was smiling, and it was such a big, beautiful smile that I was awestruck for a moment and I had to force myself to turn around and continue working. The money wasn't gonna make itself.

As I was making subsequent pitches and stackin' that paper, I would glance in the direction of the new girl and admire how them tight ass jeans she had on showed the full contours of those wide hips and thighs as she sat in the chair, learning how to pitch to potential pledgers. Every once in a while, she would glance in my direction, and at one point, our eyes met, and I swear that we made a connection.

Now I am not the handsomest man in the world, but I hold my own. Despite a few battle scars and a broken front tooth, I've never had trouble meeting or pulling women. I am always clean, my head is always freshly shaved, and I wear branded clothing that are always neat, clean, and pressed. I wear mostly sneakers, but they are always crispy. I always smell good, preferring old-school cologne like Polo. I am confident in my abilities and it shows. I walk, talk, and carry myself in a supremely confident manner at all times, so it was no surprise that the new chick was checkin' me out despite all the other males present in the room.

I am an artist. It is one of the things I learned as an inmate at various Minnesota prisons that I could use as a hustle. Damn near everybody there feels the need to maintain loving contact with their family members or their girlfriends or wives, so my homemade cards made me a lot of money. I mention this because even as I was making my pitches and checking out the new chick, I was freehand drawing and shading a rose with a black pen. When break time came, the new chick walked by me on her way out and peeped what I had drawn.

"That is beautiful," she remarked.

"Thank you," I said. "It is just a quick sketch. I can do much better."

"It is still very nice. You're very talented," she replied.

"I appreciate the compliment. My name is Nathan," I told her as I stood and offered her my hand for a shake.

"And I am Brandy," the angel introduced herself as she took my hand.

When our hands touched, a jolt of electricity shocked my hand, ran up my arm, then coursed through my whole body. I am not exaggerating in any way. It was a literal physical sensation.

And from the look of things, Brandy also experienced something similar because she jumped slightly, gave a small sigh, and her face turned red in embarrassment. She quickly released my hand and averted her eyes. It seemed as if it was love at first sight (and touch) on both of our parts.

We then proceeded outside where we continued to get to know each other. The usual questions were asked and answered. I found out that she was raised in the suburbs, had some college in her background, and had been a single mother who had gotten divorced and raised her child basically by herself before recently sending him off to college. Apparently, her ex-husband, Edward, had received a life sentence in the feds when their son was young, maybe twelve or so. Now that her son was no longer in her home, she was looking to move on in her life.

I immediately began to admire her for the strength and love she displayed throughout the years, as she had worked various jobs to support and provide for her child. The many trials and tribulations she had faced and conquered created an immediate soft spot in my heart for her.

"I must be honest with you, Ms. Brandy," I said with trepidation. Though I feared that being honest would tarnish my image and foil my chances of getting to know Brandy better, I knew that I had to make my past known if I wanted to pursue a friendship or more with her. "I am an ex-con. I've been out of prison for about a year now. I was convicted of burglary last time, but I've been down a few times for various crimes. I've been working here since my release, and

I've been working really hard to turn my life around. I write poems, and I am trying to get a book of my poems published. As you saw, I also draw, and I may also illustrate my own book depending on the circumstances. I got my own place, a whip, and I am working on my credit so I can make some moves in the future. All that being said, do you think that you can see past what I used to be and give me a chance to get to know you better as the person I am now?"

Brandy did not respond right away. She eyed me thoughtfully as she processed what I had told her. "I appreciate your honesty. I can respect that. I must admit that I think you're cute, and I can't deny my body's reaction to you. We just met, though, so I will have to think about this. But before I do, I'd like to know if you have a girl or someone that you're already talking to?"

"I do not" is all I said.

"In that case, I will allow you to walk me back inside, and we will see what happens later."

CHAPTER 5

As we reentered the building, I noticed the questioning eyes of the haters, and the jealous stares followed us relentlessly as I walked Brandy to her station and pulled out her chair for her. After she sat and got comfortable, she thanked me, and I retreated to my own station.

"What the fuck!" said Jason in the station next to mine. "Damn, dog, you ain't gonna give nobody else a chance to get at her?"

"Hell naw," I said with force. "Y'all been content fuckin' with the garbage ass broads that been here, so keep fuckin' wit' 'em. I ain't fucked with nay one of these dirty ass rats here. This one here is cut from a different cloth that is more my speed. Don't hate, congratulate!"

When work ended, I said goodbye to Brandy, as she walked by, seemingly in a hurry. I admired her backside as her cheeks jumped and jiggled like Jell-O with her quick steps. I then gathered my things and made my way out to my Aerostar minivan. I pulled out of the parking lot and took a left on Transfer Road. I drove the two blocks to University Avenue where I took another left. As I was turning, I glanced at the bus stop and saw Brandy getting on the number sixteen bus headed downtown. She saw me and waved as she got on.

I worked the 11:00 a.m. to 8:00 p.m. shifts, so by the time I got off work, most of the stores were closed or preparing to close, so things were pretty quiet on the strip and in my Frogtown neighborhood. Usually I would stop someplace to grab a bite to eat since I am a terrible cook, then I'd go home and either watch a movie, check out the highlights from the day's sporting events on ESPN, or surf the web, checking out the plethora of porn sites. That night was no different.

CHAPTER 6

But the next morning was. When I woke up, thoughts of Brandy were on my mind, and my dick was so hard that it hurt. I barely knew that girl, but she was the cause of my painful state, and I had no choice but to pull one off as I imagined those thick, luscious lips on my dick as she deepthroated me and looked me in the eye at the same damn time with those hazel eyes of hers. I imagined that she gently squeezed and rubbed my balls at the same time until I busted a fat ass nut in her mouth and then all over her face.

Despite the relief I provided for myself, I found that I was still anxious and amped-up as I moved about. My body was tight with the anticipation of seeing Brandy again, and I kept thinking about her as I followed my normal morning routine.

Throughout that day, we continued to flirt and get to know each other on our breaks. At one point, she told me she was years older than me, and I was absolutely floored! I was thirty-five at the time, which made her forty-five! This lovely lady who I had thought was a young MILF was actually an old cougar! She was still fine as hell, though, so it did not diminish my enthusiasm one bit.

And the haters continued to hate with sideways looks and whispered comments into one another's ears. Fuck 'em. Phone sales and fundraising offices are notorious for hiring ex-cons, addicts, degenerates, and misfits, or those that are all of the above, so it was to be expected. The offices themselves consist of dirty and stained carpet and chairs, dirty walls and partitions, and dirty, outdated equipment to match the majority of their employees. I had gotten used to the bullshit, so their hate and envy rolled off of me like water off a duck's back.

And this time, I did not miss the chance to offer Brandy a ride home. I am no captain-save-a-hoe type of nigga, but this beautiful lady had captivated me, and I would spend all the time with her that she would allow me to.

"Okay, Mr. Nathan. But do not presume that this means more than it does. I have not had a car for a while, and I am sick of the bus. That is the only reason that I am taking you up on your offer," she said with a coy smile.

"Agreed."

Though I am from Minneapolis, I had been living in St. Paul since I had gotten out of the halfway house. Brandy also lived in St. Paul off of Maryland and Western less than a mile away from my place, which was on Charles just off of Western. Picking her up and dropping her off weren't gonna be a hardship either way. Plus, it gave me an opportunity to be with her alone for a little while every day.

CHAPTER 7

And that was how our whirlwind relationship began. She did not allow much more interaction than our flirtation at work, the rides to and from work, and an occasional shared meal after work which she insisted on paying her fair share for. I wanted more, but she had made it quite clear that she wanted to take it slow.

Finally, I had to assert myself.

"Look here," I said as we shared a meal at Chipotle on the University of Minnesota campus, "We been flirtin' and carryin' on for three weeks now. It is obvious that you are diggin' me as much as I am diggin' you, so why are we still slow rollin'? I don't expect you to give it up right away, and we sure ain't gonna move in together anytime soon, but will you at least allow me to take you out sometime?"

She looked at me speculatively as she took a sip of soda to calm the burn of the hot sauce that was on her burrito. Her lips on the straw gave me a flashback of the fantasy I had about her the morning after I met her, and I began to get hard. I had to force myself to look her in the eye. I was hard as diamond by then, and my dick was beginning to hurt as it throbbed incessantly in the confines of my boxer shorts.

"I suppose we could do that. What do you have in mind?" she asked.

"This is about you. What do you want to do?"

"I want to go to the Mall of America and walk around 'till I find me a nice outfit, then you can take me out to eat at one of the restaurants there, and we can go on some of the rides," she said.

"The Mall of America it is," I agreed.

*****

From there, it took off like a rocket, as they say. As we began to get more acquainted and our contact and affection began to increase, it was getting harder and harder to work with her. I began to want to grab her and kiss her on sight or squeeze on her fat booty or hold her hand, but that would have been very unprofessional even in such a dirty work environment, so I had to control my urges 'till we were all alone.

It did not take long for us to fall head over heels in love. When she finally allowed me to make love to her, it was magic. The pussy was as tight as a virgin's because she hadn't had sex in about four years. During one of our previous conversations, she had told me that she had been with one other man for about two years after her baby daddy had gone to prison, but when he got too controlling and verbally abusive, she left him and had been on her own for the past four years with no sex. If I had any doubts previously regarding her claims, they evaporated immediately as I struggled to enter that hot, extremely tight hole. It felt like home as I was finally able to get up in there. I had not been in a pussy that tight since my first love, and I lost our virginity to each other at the age of thirteen.

I was sprung. She had me doing things that I never really did before. I would place a single red rose on the passenger seat of my van when I went to pick her up. I would be all hugged up with her in public. I would hold her hand. I would get jealous if other guys looked at her. These are all of the things that I had previously considered sucka-for-love type of shit.

All that from a guy who once fucked his girl's cousin right next to her as she was passed out, unaware that such treachery was taking place so close to her. I think her cousin had even draped her leg over her inert body as I tore that ass up.

And all that from a man who let the mother of his girlfriend at the time suck his dick in the kitchen while she was in the basement washing our clothes. Then her mom had the nerve to talk to her and smile all up in her face with my dick and cum all over her breath. Dirty bitch.

There are many more examples, but you get the point. I was terrible to women before my last incarceration. I was mentally, verbally, and physically abusive as well as a consummate cheater. I was a product of my environment at the time. Lucky for us, I had gained a new perspective and understanding of right and wrong during my last incarceration and I yearned to change, or we never would have stood a chance. I had been working diligently to consciously rid myself of my abusive ways, and I was able to return her love and affection in full.

CHAPTER 8

It is here that I will give you a little background so that you can understand the person I was, the person I am, and the person that I want to be. It will also help you to understand why this potential relationship is so important to me.

After one of the times my mother had abandoned me and I was sent to a foster home, she came to get me, having once again convinced the courts that she was able to care for me. I was eight years old at the time. She married a man that she did not love just because she did not want to be alone. That was the reason that she gave me years later before I cut her off. The man she married was lazy and abusive, an addict and an alcoholic—just a plain piece of shit in general.

There is one particular day that I will always remember. For some reason, it is distinct in my mind out from the hundreds of other times that I was abused.

It was a cloudy day. It hadn't rained, but it was sure to; I could smell it in the air. Whatever had set my stepfather off was sure to have been something small or petty, as it always was.

SLAP! My stepfather slapped me hard across my face. SLAP! His hand came across the other way in a vicious backhand. He did this repeatedly as he screamed and yelled in my face, telling me how worthless I was and how I would never be shit. As he abused me verbally and physically, spittle flew out of his mouth and sprayed me in the face. His breath, hot and rancid from drinking copious amounts of cheap wine and from smoking much weed, washed over my face and assaulted my nostrils, almost causing me to gag. My mother, who usually played on the sidelines and watched each abusive scene unfold, was screaming for him to stop. He ignored her.

Suddenly, to everybody's surprise—including even her own, I suspect—my mother tried to step in between us and stop the assault. While my stepfather was slapping me back and forth with his right hand, he had an iron grip on my right arm with his left to make sure that I couldn't get away, so her intervention was made difficult. She tried to pry his grip loose, but he was too strong, his strength from being an amateur boxer still somewhat formidable despite his overindulgence in weed and alcohol.

My stepfather's reaction was swift and violent. Releasing my arm, as if to say, "If this is what you wanted, this is what you will get," he delivered a powerful backhand across her pale, freckled face. My mother is very white, of Scandinavian descent, with almost-white blonde hair, so by the time she fell back into the wall with a thud then bounced off of it, there was already a backhand print appearing on her face.

My stepfather then pounced on her quickly, delivering the same type of blows that he had been administering to me only seconds before. My male instincts urged me to go to her rescue, but my thoroughly abused mind, body, heart, and soul prevented me from doing so, seeing as how she had let the abuse of myself continue for so long unchecked. In a sick way, I was pleased

Suddenly, another surprise. In the midst of the blows, I saw a white hand reach out and up. The paper-white hand was formed into a claw. My mother then dug her long claws into my stepfather's face and pulled down forcefully, breaking through the skin and digging four shallow trenches down the side of his face.

Then the other hand came up and struck as quick as a cat. My stepfather was caught off guard and was slow to react, allowing her to get in three or four blows. The shock in his eyes and the scared look on his face were and are priceless to me. He had been beating us for so long and with such little resistance that he never expected either of us to fight back.

Then his boxer's instincts kicked in, and he threw his hands up to cover his face, stepping back and pivoting as he did so. He saved his face from much more damage when he did so because my mother had no intention of stopping. But she was still on him like flies on shit, scratching and clawing at anything available with a fury that I would have never thought that she could possess.

At some point, my stepfather decided that his best chance for survival was to use his superior strength to subdue her. So he took his hands down from his face and, with lightning quickness, put her in a bear hug, clenching like most fighters do when they are tired of getting their ass whooped. My mother then tried to bite his face, but he was pretty good at that bobbin' and weavin' shit, so he avoided getting a chunk taken out of his face or something.

He held her fast, telling her to stop, and she continued to struggle. It took a few moments, but eventually, she calmed down. He did not let her go until she agreed that it was over. Being cautious, he held on to her for a few moments more until he felt the tension go out of her.

At some point, he left. After a while, when she was sure that he would not be back anytime soon, she came and told me that we would be leaving. We each packed a few things. When my mother realized that he had taken her house key, she quickly formulated a plan.

There was a balcony attached to the upper level of the duplex, and that was where we lived. She had me lock all the doors and windows, go out on the porch, climb over the rail, then hang down and drop. She was supposed to catch me, but I think she got scared, despite my small frame. When I landed, I instinctively fell backward as soon as my feet touched the ground, allowing my butt to take the brunt of the force rather than my knees, then flipped backward and on to my knees. One of my mother's relatives, whom I had never met, picked us up, and we went to stay with her and her husband in the roach-and-mouse-infested projects for about a week or so. Then my stepfather convinced her that he had changed and that it would never happen again for the umpteenth time. That was a lie of course.

CHAPTER 9

My stepfather was the main male figure in my life. Not only was he abusive but he was also a bum, my mother and he depending on welfare and food stamps along with the occasional drug dealing to get by. This, despite the fact that they were both able-bodied adults. His example is what I learned and the cause of what I became.

Throughout the rest of my childhood and up until my last prison bit, my anger and resentment were nuclear. My blood was always boiling, and I was always at the point of snapping. When I did snap, I was not only abusive verbally and physically but destructive as well. I would beat my girlfriends' asses at the most miniscule of slights, punch holes in walls, and destroy our property. Many new phones, TVs, and radios had to be repurchased over the years.

And, of course, I was always high on marijuana, but that was frequently accompanied by coke, alcohol, various pills like Klonopin, Xanax, Wellbutrin, and such. I went through life in a mindless fog, doing anything and everything to cover up the pain, anger, and insecurity that mirrored that of my stepfather's life. The fact that I had become just like him only magnified my feelings, and they became more corrosive.

Being an addict, I could not hold a job, which put more pressure on the women who were dumb enough to date me even after being warned. So I had to resort to criminal activities like robbery, burglary, and the occasional drug dealing to survive. When those opportunities did not present themselves, I would take my women's money whether they allowed me to or not. If they expressed their displeasure with my actions, I would beat their asses.

Needless to say, I was in and out of prisons throughout the great state of Minnesota over the years. Each and every time, I would blame those same women for abandoning me. I was unable to empathize with them because I would then have to face the fact that I was a horrible person in all ways, the same exact person that I had come to loathe over the years. The only difference I could see between my stepfather and I was that he was deathly afraid of my father and his reputation, and twice I had seen him back down from other grown men. He was truly a coward to the bone. Me, I was always welcoming of a good scrap. It was another outlet for the anger festering inside of me.

CHAPTER 10

The reason that I have revealed all of this to you is so that you can understand the mind-set that I once had. During my last incarceration, something made me do some soul-searching. I think that maybe I was just sick and tired of being miserable, of being thought of as less than human by the so-called "normal" society, and of causing pain to others for so long. I knew that with my IQ of 170 (the prison tested me), I could be anything that I wanted to be.

It was at that time that I started writing poems. Those poems were idealistic poems of love and companionship and all that comes with those like romance, and physical, mental, and emotional intimacy. I expressed my respect, admiration, adoration, and yearning to provide the best relational experience I longed for when I finally found the love of my life. I knew that were I to rid myself of my baggage, then I could be a very nice marital partner to the lady lucky enough to receive all my pent-up love.

I had never been able to love anybody because I did not love myself. As time passed and I began reading self-help books pertaining to things like forgiveness, spirituality, and entrepreneurship, my thinking began to change. I began to meditate and started clearing my mind of the past, focusing mostly on forgiveness because I instinctively knew that it was going to be the key to me breaking a vicious cycle so that I can utilize my God-given intelligence to live up to my potential. I knew that it was necessary to rid myself of the baggage that was holding me down so that I could make room for a brighter, happier, and more productive future.

As my knowledge, confidence, and understanding grew, so did my urge to love and be loved. I realized that the misogynistic, crass individual that I once was an abomination in the Creator's eyes. With every book I read, including the Bible, and every documentary of instructional video that I watched in the prison library, I began to understand love in a limited way and to comprehend that love is the total opposite of all that I have ever been and all that I've ever known. That helped me to formulate in my mind my ideal mate, what I wanted to give her, and what I expected in return.

Miss Brandy seemed to fit the picture. I had in my mind an image of an ideal woman, and she was the one whom I had been talking about in my poems and prose. Our interactions were as smooth as butter, and she was graceful, charming, enchanting, intelligent, strong, and determined to make something of herself now that she didn't have anyone to take care of and look after other than herself.

And she brought out the best in me. She made me want to love her with all of my heart, protect her, guide her, and spoil her. She understood my dreams, wants, and needs, and she was agreeable to becoming successful with me as a team. It also didn't hurt that she was fine as hell.

CHAPTER 11

Eventually, the time came when we decided to move in together. As we were looking for a place, a friend of hers who owned a double bungalow on the east side of St. Paul informed us that one of her units had recently become available. We pooled our money together and paid the first and last month's rent and the damage deposit. It was already partly furnished, and we just had to purchase a few additional items along with dishes, towels, rags, bed linens, toiletries, and some odds and ends. Being a mother and a nurturer, Brandy wasted no time in making our new house a home with her decorative ability and a woman's touch. It was very comfortable and cozy by the time she was finished.

Once we were properly settled and a little time had passed, we began to look to the future. We began to save money in both a joint account and in separate accounts. Our credit scores were improving with each bill paid on time. Discussions regarding our financial future ensued. We began to explore areas of interest such as investment opportunities, businesses that we would be interested in owning, and rental property ownership.

Then there were the discussions about what steps we would take to accomplish our goals like the need to continue to build our credit, what classes and seminars we could attend, and what degrees we would need to pursue to gain the knowledge necessary to make our endeavors successful. Our future looked bright indeed.

CHAPTER 12

But as the old saying goes, "if you want to make God laugh, tell him your plans." Brandy and I had plans to live happily ever after, but the good Lord had his own plans. Disaster struck suddenly and unexpectedly one morning in the form of a bout of irritable bowel syndrome or IBS. I had had bouts previously, but it bad been more than five years since the last one, and I thought I was already past that.

I started vomiting frequently, and I was always nauseous but at the same time very hungry. I experienced debilitating stomach cramps and pangs with large buildups of acid in my stomach that burned like the fires of hell and torched my esophagus and throat every time I vomited. I could hold down no food or water, and I became dehydrated on top of everything else.

I hung in there as best as I could at work, but eventually I had to call in sick and head to the hospital. I was dangerously dehydrated, and I had to be hooked up to an intravenous drip to get much-needed fluids into my body. The normal battery of tests was run, and just like the hundreds of other times I had been in various emergency rooms and at scheduled clinic appointments, the doctors could not figure out what was wrong with me. IBS can be a generic diagnosis, and just like before, all the doctors could do was prescribe medication for nausea (not that the ones they prescribed at the time worked all that well), acid reflux, and pain, and hope for the best.

The nausea and acid reflux medications did the trick for a short while, but my body soon developed a tolerance for them, and they were no longer effective. The nausea and acid reflux returned and so did the dehydration and hunger pangs. I was back to the emergency room for a much-needed IV drip to rehydrate me and prescriptions for some more expensive and soon-to-be useless medication. One was a rectal medication. As humiliating as it was for me, oral medication was no longer an option because I could not keep it down. The rectal medication and the new acid reflux medication were kind of expensive. I was not insured at the time, but I needed the relief, so I gladly paid cash for them. I was in such bad shape that the doctor gave me an excuse slip to miss two weeks of work.

When I dropped by work to give my boss the doctor's note, he was not in the least thrilled. He had already been making snide little remarks about needing my seat to be filled so I could make the company money. Everybody knows that the fundraisers actually get the lion's share of the money that they raise. His comments stayed with me throughout the week, and I returned to work a few days early.

Bad idea. An hour after starting, I was in the bathroom vomiting copiously and very loudly. The medication was not working once again. A supervisor from another department happened to be in the bathroom at the time, and he went and reported my condition to my own supervisor. When I returned, he gave me a knowing look, and when I asked to go home for the day, he sent me home permanently.

I knew that that shit was against the law, so the next day, I mustered up the courage and energy needed to make my way to the Department of Human Rights in downtown St. Paul to file a complaint. Their investigation came to naught because my supervisor lied and said that he fired me for a verbal disagreement that I had with a supervisor from another department. I wanted to go over there and beat his ass, but I just didn't have the strength.

CHAPTER 13

Brandy had been an angel throughout the first part of that harrowing ordeal, but after a while, her true colors started to show. She couldn't understand my illness and its sudden appearance. When the medications failed several times and my trips to the emergency room and to clinics became more frequent, her nurturing manner started to slowly disappear. I could see the love being drained away by my illness like the sands in an hourglass and replaced by resentment like how the sand is replaced by so much empty air. There were times when I would be on the floor writhing in pain or curled up in a ball moaning, and I swear I'd see a look of disgust on her face.

Then when my last check was gone, she was solely responsible for paying the bills, car note, insurance, and the price of my medication. This pressure allowed her weakness and insecurity to show. They were manifested in her constant yapping, whining, complaining, blaming, and attempts to emasculate me. If I hadn't been in such a weak state, I probably would have slapped the dogshit out of her to shut her ass up despite my new resolve. Never would I have accepted such disrespect if I had been well.

"Nathan, I cannot continue to do this," she stated bluntly one day as I lay on the kitchen floor because it was cooler than suffering in the bed. I had been vomiting into a bucket and sweating heavily, so the cold floor was a relief. "I didn't sign up for this. I am not your mother, and I don't want to keep caring for you as if I am."

Needless to say, I was in a complete shock. I knew that my illness had been hard on her, and she had been distant for some time, but never in a million years would I have thought that she would act like that. It was unfathomable to me that that sweet, strong, nurturing, caring woman whom I had come to know and love with all of my heart would transform so completely into such a bitch.

"What the fuck do you mean?" I rasped. My throat was raw and sore from so much throwing up, and I could barely talk. "I did not ask for this any more than you did, and I can't help being sick. What is wrong with you?"

"You are all sick and shit, and I have to work full-time, take care of you, and listen to you throwing up all the time with your whinin' and moanin' and all that. I just can't take this shit anymore," she said coldly as she looked down on me with undisguised contempt in her eyes.

"I can't help this shit, Brandy. This ain't the first time this has happened. It will pass eventually."

"When, Nathan? How much longer do I have to deal with this shit? Not only are you sick and as helpless as a baby, but you aren't working, and I'm paying all the bills by myself! This shit ain't fair to me!" she exclaimed.

"Well, what the fuck do you want me to do? There really isn't anything I CAN do except wait it out."

All the stress and activity made me nauseous, and I leaned over my bucket and vomited up all the acid that had accumulated. It burned painfully, and it effectively cut our conversation short.

As I lay there recovering from that last bout, my mind was divided between my pain and discomfort and my recent conversation with my so-called love. It seemed that there was a fatal flaw in the woman I had once thought was so perfect for me, the woman whom I had been seriously contemplating spending the rest of my life with. I was completely lost and dumbfounded. How could I have missed that flaw in her?

CHAPTER 14

Over the next few days, we barely spoke to each other, and things were very tense between us. When the rent was due and the bills began arriving, she paid it all, but then we were strapped for cash. She was walking around with her face all scrunched up and her lips poked out. I wondered if she acted like that when her kids were sick.

"Damn, girl, why you walkin' around lookin' like that and ignorin' a nigga? All that funny actin' shit isn't helpin' the situation none."

"We are damn near broke, Nathan," she replied somewhat venomously. "This check to check shit is not what I'm used to with a man in the house. I struggled when me and my kids were on our own, but I should not have to struggle when there are two of us that should be contributing to this household. My daddy always took good care of me and my mother, and my kid's daddy always made sure that we never wanted for nothin'!"

"Well, go and get back with that nigga then!" I yelled. "Oh, that's right, he's in prison for the rest of his life. So I guess he won't be taking care of you no damn more."

Lucky for me, I was somewhat in a state of remission at that point. One of the doctors had prescribed Compazine for nausea and Protonix for acid reflux, and they were working miracles. They allowed me to be able to defend myself and not be in the vulnerable position I always seemed to be in when she started in on me with her bullshit. Or so I thought until her next remarks!

"Well, at least he has an excuse! Them white folks got him locked in a cage. But you're free and still can't do shit! You're a weak excuse for a man!" she yelled.

I recoiled as if she had physically slapped me. Her words had hurt me to the core. In my mind's eye, I saw myself punching her in the jaw and shattering that joint as I knocked her cold the fuck out. In reality, I just stopped and stared at her unbelievingly with my mouth wide open.

She seemed to realize that she had gone too far, but once the words were spoken, they couldn't be retracted. The pain and feelings of betrayal she had caused registered plainly on my face. Nothing she could say after that could ever assuage those.

"I am *sooooooo* sorry, Nathan. I did not mean it. I am just feeling under so much pressure tight now," she tried to apologize as she tried to hug me.

I stepped back from her attempted embrace without responding. I just stared at her for a moment before I turned away and left to go for a drive. I knew then and there that if we somehow made it through our situation, things would never be the same between us. Not for me anyway.

So we went through the motions. I was feeling better from the medication and was able to move around a little bit more with hardly any effects from my illness. Brandy alternated between somewhat detached and somewhat caring. The bills began to pile up, and I was feeling the pressure not only from her but from myself. I had tried to change my life and be a good man and a positive member of the regular society, but it just wasn't working out. My own body had betrayed me. God had betrayed me. Brandy had betrayed me. Never before had I felt so low.

But what Brandy said had a ring of truth to it. I was not living up to my manly responsibilities no matter what the cause. My male ego was large, and my illness, combined with her words, had bruised it to the fullest. I had to figure something out.

CHAPTER 15

I was caught between a rock and a hard place. I needed money, and I needed to get this bitch off my back, but I couldn't work, so what was I to do? I could move around at that point, but I was still kind of weak. That, plus even when that bitch was at work, I could hear her voice in my head taunting me. It was like her voice was my own damn thoughts. This bitch was driving me crazy, and she wasn't even there!

Then one day, I was lying in bed, chillin', and watching the news which had reported three bank robberies throughout the Twin Cities the previous day. Notes were used in all of them, and all of the perpetrators were still at large. Two of the robbers were suspected of multiple robberies, and all were still unidentified. How could that be? My interest was piqued, and as I paid close attention, I saw that the images caught by the cameras were either blurry, grainy, or both. I also noticed that those cats never looked directly at the camera.

Bling! A big, bright ass light bulb suddenly appeared above my head. I had what I thought at the time was a bright idea. Shit, if they could do it and get away with it, then so could I! If I could rob just one bank, I was sure to get enough money to cure my financial woes and get that naggin' ass bitch off my ass.

It took me a few days to muster up the courage though. This was a new level of risk for me, and I knew that it would take a giant set of cojones to walk up in them white folks' bank and take their money. Cats get less time for killing. One time, I saw a drunk driver on the news that had killed a Minnesota State Patrol officer and only got two and a half years. This, even though he had several previous arrests and convictions for drunk driving. But them white folks sure as hell don't play when it comes to their scratch.

One morning, after a hellacious night of Brandy's incessant nagging, whining, and complaining, I decided that I would do ANYTHING short of killing her ass to shut her the fuck up. I got up after she went to work, and I prepared to do the damn thang. Everybody who knows me knows that I wear a moderately full goatee with my beautiful bald head. That morning, I shaved my goatee completely off and donned a Minnesota Twins baseball cap. This was a great disguise since I rarely ever wore a baseball cap. People who knew me would never recognize me on TV with the poor images taken by the bank's cameras—not even my own family.

I then put on two sets of clothes. Since it was a mild winter day, this would not be uncomfortable or cause any problems as long as the clothing wasn't too thick. I grabbed a pair of black knit gloves, put them in my pocket, then stepped out into a day filled with sunshine and promise, and walked to Arcade and Maryland avenues to catch the number sixty-four bus as I had planned. I took that to downtown St. Paul where I then got on the E16 bus to take me to my preplanned destination. And that is where this story began.

CHAPTER 16

I wish it had ended there. I am an addict by nature and genetics, so that was never really a possibility despite my intentions. When I got to the crib, I went straight to the bedroom where I counted the money and separated the bills into like denominations on the bed. My haul was $5,270. I put $500 aside for emergency purposes, $100 in my pocket for some squares, something to eat, and gas money, and I left the rest on the bed as I went about my business.

When Brandy got home, I was chillin' on the couch watching *Get Rich or Die Tryin'* for the umpteenth time. After a less-than-cordial greeting, she made her way to the bedroom to change out of her work clothes. A few seconds later, I heard a loud, startled exclamation, and she hurriedly returned to the living room.

"Nathan, where did all of this money come from?" she asked sharply with her hands on her hips.

"I could tell you, but then I'd have to kill you," I joked to try to ease the tension.

"Stop playing with me, Nathan James. This is no joke. What have you gotten yourself into?" she asked insistently.

"Baby, you don't wanna know. The less you know, the better, for your own sake. You been bitchin' and complainin' about my lack of financial contribution, so just accept it for what it is."

"That money could not have come from anything good. I refuse to deal with it."

"You didn't refuse to deal with your baby daddy's dope money. You always sayin' how he took such good care of y'all. And you don't even know where that money came from, and you actin' like you're too good to spend it. I coulda got a loan from the bank or something for all you know." I looked at her pointedly and she rolled her eyes.

"Bae, I am not stupid," she said as she snapped her neck. "And look where Edward ended up. That man will never see the light of day again. I don't want that for you. You know that I know that whatever you did to get that money ain't right and that if you get caught, there will be hell to pay. And I don't want to be seen as an accomplice to anything you've done."

Exasperated, I replied, "If you'd stop askin' so many damn questions and just accept it for what it is, you wouldn't have shit to worry about. Let me worry about this. I got this. Since you've known me, you've known that when I say 'I got this,' I mean it with no reservation. If you don't know shit, you can't be an accomplice to shit! We have the means in that room to pay all our bills and to even prepay a couple of months of bills to see us through until I get back on my feet. What's wrong with that? And I ain't admittin' to no wrongdoing anyways."

Brandy looked at me skeptically, but I could see that she was calculating the pros and cons of becoming involved with the money. Eventually she sighed, gave me an embarrassed half smile, and took my hand. "Okay, I know this will get us out of a bind, so I accept it. But I want to make myself perfectly clear. Whatever you've done must stop. This cannot be a regular occurrence. We are straight now. How much is there, by the way?"

That night, we made love like nothing bad had ever happened between us. That head and that pussy was so good that I almost forgot the betrayal she had perpetrated against me. Almost.

CHAPTER 17

Two days later, the money had been spent as we had agreed upon. We were almost down to the $500 I had stashed. She didn't know about that and was already looking ahead to future complications financially. She began runnin' her fuckin' mouth like there was no tomorrow. She damn near made me relapse. I had thought about going to buy a $300 ounce of that fire and some Hen Dogg to help me cope, but instead I relinquished the $500 to shut her the fuck up.

Another bank job was imminent. I was just consciously realizing what my subconscious already knew. Not only did I have to recapture that indescribable feeling but I was still physically weak, with no job prospects or ways to earn money. That last reason is all the justification I needed to begin mentally preparing myself for the next lick. A man has got to survive and provide, don't he? Ain't that in the constitution or some shit? In my mind, my instant addiction had nothing to do with it.

So five days later, using the same "disguise" and a pair of non-prescription glasses that were way different than my regular pair and contacts in my eyes (because I am as blind as a bat), it was, once again, on. The method was the same, and I even took the bus again to make sure that there would be no description of my van or my license plate number. Smart, huh? The haul was less $4,130, but once again, there were no problems. It couldn't get any easier to make a few stacks.

This time, there were no delinquent bills. Still, though, I set aside $1,500 to break Brandy off so I wouldn't have to hear her mouth, and with the rest, I bought a couple of fly outfits at Macy's with some shoes to match, and I bought a pair of Vikings tickets for the last game of the season. I wanted to see them kick the Packers' asses!

CHAPTER 18

I knew that if I wanted to continue in my new profession, I would have to start using better, more elaborate disguises. Sure, my family and friends didn't recognize me on the evening news, but it was only a matter of time before a teller or bank manager recognized a peculiarity or trait from one of those images and get a silent alarm, or a so-called friend or family member saw me in a recognizable posture or position, put two and two together, and allowed their greed to make them call them folds on me so that they could collect any reward that was offered for my arrest and conviction.

I found a costume shop online that was located in Madison, Wisconsin, which is not too far from where I was but far enough that the Twin Cities news cycles would not be full of stories about me. So off I went to Cheesehead land. I told the naïve young clerk there that I suspected that my wife was cheating on me and that I did not have the money to hire a private investigator so I would need to collect the evidence myself. I wove a story of such sadness, heartbreak, pain, and betrayal that she spent damn near an hour showing me how to apply different types of mustaches, beards, and other accessories such as makeup, hats, glasses, and shoes with lifts to help me significantly alter my appearance.

Over the next ten robberies, I employed those tactics well. Watching the news, one would have thought that there was a whole band of thieves out there robbing them joints. I monitored the news religiously and was amazed at how different I looked in each grainy picture. I had to remind myself that all those pictures were actually of ME.

CHAPTER 19

My hauls had gotten bigger (in the $7,000–$10,000 range) because I had started going into the banks later, around 3:00 p.m., when the banks would be putting enough in the drawers to cover customer transactions when they got off work. I also started robbing mostly on Fridays, which was payday. A bonus to that was at that time, most police officers were on their way to shift change, and response times were slower.

At first, Brandy didn't like coming home to all the paper on the bed, paper she just knew had to be ill-gotten, but with all the bitchin' she had previously done, what could she really say? Especially when she started mentally spending those crisp new big faces I had put in her hand?

Money is the root of all evil, but it is also a hell of an elixir. Though Brandy had her misgivings, she was starting to warm up to me, and she even had a kind word or two. *Funky bitch*, I thought as I counted all the teeth she was showing me one day. My love for her was still strong, but at the front of my mind was the fact that she had basically kicked me when I was down instead of helping a nigga up. I gave her no indication that I had anything other than love for her, but feelings of abandonment and betrayal were there nonetheless.

As time progressed, the turnaround in Brandy's attitude was astounding. The more time that passed, the more I was actually starting to believe that she actually and truly loved me again. For allegedly being such a square, she took to the comforts that my criminal endeavors provided like how a fish takes to water. As she had previously with her ex-husband.

She had no problem thoroughly enjoying expensive dinners at upscale restaurants, spending weekends at high-priced hotels, jewelry, and all the other perks. Gone were the attitudes and the nagging, and I was beginning to feel as if she were the woman I had originally fallen in love with. She even went out of her way to do freaky shit that she had never done before. Never had a woman throw my legs up in the air and start licking my asshole and balls while expertly stroking my cock. I was resistant at first because I felt gay as hell letting her do it, but her hot, moist mouth and tongue quickly eliminated any resistance. Her actions, subsequent to the onset of my illness, had created much doubt and resentment, but our renewed love gave me one more solid reason to go out and get that money.

CHAPTER 20

But it was getting harder and harder to find banks that were cop- and security guard-free that were accessible by bus. After thirteen successful robberies by bus, I had to consider using my whip. I had serious reservations about that because I figured that my chances of getting caught increased because someone could get a description of my van or provide the cops with a license plate number. One look around my crib—at the new furniture, my high-tech entertainment system—and thinking about the newfound happiness that the money had brought to Brandy and I, and all doubts disappeared completely.

And so I deviated from my normally effective routine. Luck or God—or whatever it was—was with me the first two times. I sort of followed my old routine in that I had parked a little way away then changed my appearance on the way back to the car after the deed was done. The altered appearance combined with my nonchalant attitude made me look as if I had belonged and ensured that I did not attract any undue attention or that I did not stick in anyone's mind.

But whoever said that the third time is a charm is a damn liar. From the moment I got up and started getting ready to drive to my next job, shit went wrong. When I went to take a shower right after I woke up, there was no hot water because the water heater was malfunctioning according to the caretaker. Then once I was ready, I couldn't find my "lucky" gloves that I wore on every job, and lastly, I had to get a jump from one of my neighbors because I had left my lights on all night. You would think that someone would have said something.

In my mind, I told myself that it wasn't a good day to follow through with my plans, but my addiction to the adrenaline rush and that little devil on my shoulder made it impossible to pay attention to my instincts and the warning bells they were setting off.

The robbery itself was fucked up from the moment I set foot in the bank. That three o'clock or so time frame I had been using in Minneapolis and St. Paul was perfect because most people were still at work at that time or struggling with rush-hour traffic, but out in the suburb of Burnsville, a short distance from where Highways 5 and 13 intersect, shit was jumpin'. There were people everywhere. And the bank that I had found online and cased earlier in the week was no different at 3:00 p.m. here. The bank was full. My first mind was to turn my yella ass right around, but once again, I ignored my instincts and went ahead and tried to complete the job at hand.

Usually I am able to proceed from the island containing the various slips and applications straight to the teller's window, but that time, I had to wait in a short line. As I waited, my body and mind were screaming at me to abandon my plan and vacate the premises as soon as possible. Outwardly, I appeared to be my normal cool, calm, and collected self.

When my turn came, I approached the teller's window, and I handed him my note. It was a brotha, so I thought that I had gotten lucky. He read my note, pursed his lips, then looked at me. I could tell right away by the gleam in his eye and the way that he raised that one stupid eyebrow that he was gonna be on some bullshit.

"Don't play," I told him quietly and menacingly.

"I won't," he responded then started passing me the paper.

Suddenly that fool just up and slammed the drawer shut. I was about to threaten him, but I didn't even have a pistol, so how much of a threat could I have really been? Instead, I finally listened to myself and got the fuck out of there. I hit the door running and didn't stop until I reached my car.

I had parked two blocks away with a suitable alley along the route for me to pull my Superman routine, but I could hear sirens in the distance, so I panicked and headed straight to my car, bypassing the alley.

Because that little sellout bitch had hit a silent alarm to protect them white folks' money, sirens were already blaring in the distance and I had to alter my regular routine and hope that nobody fingered my car. I vowed that I would come back at a later date and make his punk Oreo ass see the error of his ways in a very painful, traumatic, and prolonged manner.

CHAPTER 21

I got away at the time, but dig this: some snow had accumulated, and there were piles of it in the small parking lot where I had parked. My dumb ass had parked with my front end kissing one of those piles, and an imprint of my license plate was embedded in one of them. It was very clear for the FBI investigators. Because I didn't get a chance to change my clothes and appearance, it wasn't hard for the investigators to find witnesses to point out my escape route and to even follow my getaway on cameras placed throughout the shopping district. They even had a picture of me getting into the car.

Before FBI agents in conjunction with the St. Paul police conducted a raid on my spot and arrested Brandy and me the next morning, they had all of their ducks in a row. Once they ran my license plate number and got my name and address, they then procured my driver's license photo. They compared my picture to pictures from robberies over the past few months or so, and lo and behold, two of the suspects matched my general appearance and build. It turns out that in the second bank I had robbed, I looked directly into the camera for some stupid reason. Even with my semi-altered appearance that I had first utilized and the poor quality of the camera pictures, a full-frontal view of my handsome face pretty much sealed my fate.

I had no knowledge of the license imprint in the snowbank, but I was worried nonetheless. REALLY worried. I knew that the possibility existed that someone had seen which car I had entered, maybe even my plates. I stayed up all night pacing, worrying, and contemplating getting drunk to ease my nerves. I said many prayers as I paced and was even able to sit down and doze off a time or two.

It is common knowledge in the Twin Cities that the task forces of Minneapolis and St. Paul conduct their raids at exactly 6:05 a.m., on the dot. When 6:10 rolled around, I began to relax and I was anticipating a long, peaceful sleep. After I brushed my teeth and took a quick shower, I swallowed two allergy pills to help me sleep then lay down next to Brandy's fine ass. She had slept the night away blissfully unaware of the chaos and havoc that we had nearly been subjected to.

CHAPTER 22

J ust as I was falling into a deep sleep, there was a loud BANG then shouts of "POLICE! SEARCH WARRANT!" followed by the sounds of heavy, hurried footsteps rapidly approaching the bedroom. Before I could sit halfway up, I was struck hard in the chest with the butt of a shotgun by a black-clad officer in combat gear with FBI emblazoned across the chest in large white letters. A split second later, the business end of that same shotgun was about one inch from my face, and I was told that if I moved, the cop would blow my head off. I stayed as still as a statue.

Brandy woke up with a scream then shrank back against me quickly as the ghastly sight of those officers surrounding us with various types of weapons pointed at us registered in her mind. She is a very smart lady, and despite her supposed ignorance regarding my activities over the past few months, she knew what it was. I told her not to say a word until she spoke to a lawyer right before we were both yanked forcefully from our bed by multiple sets of strong arms and hands, manhandled, and thrown roughly to the floor to be handcuffed.

One officer had his knee on my neck, one had his knee in the middle of my back, and both had their full weight on me. My head was turned to the side with my face flat on the ground, so I had a clear view of Brandy. The look on her face was priceless to me. I enjoyed the look of pain and humiliation on her face so much that I forgot about the pain and discomfort that the officers were inflicting on me. At that time, I felt that she had driven me to do what I had done, and I felt that she deserved to be there on that floor with me.

I knew that she had no idea about what was in store for her and that she would face mad ostracism, suspicion, and rejection for years to come, a non-penal sentence of her own to coincide with the one that I was sure to receive. It didn't matter that she really had nothing to do with it. Everybody thought that she had to have known what I was up to since she had obviously helped me savor the fruits of my endeavors.

CHAPTER 23

Of course Brandy provided as much info as she could when she was threatened with charges. She gave them approximate dates of when I turned up with large sums of cash, but that was all she knew because I didn't trust that little bitch enough to confide in her. I don't think they could have really done too much to her, but the feds can be quite convincing, especially when they mention their 98% conviction rate. So she did her best to spill her guts.

Despite my stupid decisions, I am no dummy. They couldn't positively link me to fourteen of the robberies because of my various disguises, but they had me for the three. Them folks said my criminal background put me at a category six, the highest category, and that my offense level was thirty-two. On their grid, that put me at a possible sentence of 210–262 months. Then they told me that if I plead guilty to the three robberies, they could actually tie me to that. They would give me a three-point reduction in my level, which would put me at a possible sentence of 151–188 months. I'd be charged for one bank robbery, and the others would be considered relevant conduct. I was playing games about signing at first, but when they showed me that picture of me with the full-frontal view, I quickly asked, "Where do I sign?" See, I ain't no dummy.

Brandy stuck it out for a little while. In truth, I hated that bitch more for basically abandoning me and resenting me when I was sick than for ratting me out with what little information that she had. I had a little money put away when I got arrested, and a subpoena was issued for the safe deposit box I had at the bank (which was ironic), and the money I had there was confiscated. Brandy's worthless ass was all that I had. I knew that she was gonna break bad because that was the type of bitch she was, so I played the role and got as much money out of her as I could before she left me high and dry.

CHAPTER 24

And so here I sit in a United States penitentiary. My violent past ensured that this would be no cushy ride in an FCI (medium security), or the less restrictive low security facilities and camps, and that my 151 months would be hard. Despite my tendency to duck suckas, trouble came looking for me, and I had to kill one of my own black brothas (you'll probably read about it later), and I've lost a chunk of my precious good time. Thank God the nigga attacked me on camera and the feds refused to press charges. I did spend thirty months locked down in the SHU (the hole) and the SMU (Special Management Unit, which is similar to the hole but with a lot of fake ass programming involved) as a result of that incident.

But such is prison life. We just gotta roll with the punches. Jobs are hard to come by in the feds, and the ones that are available don't pay shit, but I am a motherfuckin' hustler, so I get what I need. I write, draw, and make the best homemade taffy in the feds, so my locker and my account stay full. I am now on the downside of my sentence, and I pray that I can get out of here without having to kill a nigga or getting killed myself.

I do what I can to make sure that I never come back to prison. I spent my SMU time productively, and I spend my time in population doing exactly the same thing. I stay busy with my various hustles, I make it a point to stay sucka-free, and I consciously work on practicing my new principles of faith, love, forgiveness, patience, positivity, and perseverance. I read books along those lines as well as books on prosperity. And last but not the least, I have formulated a vigorous workout routine that keeps me physically and mentally fit. I just can't do this shit anymore.

EPILOGUE

I n the end, my situations and the way I handled them boil down to just one thing: choices. I made the choices to rob bands and commit the many crimes that I've committed. There were most definitely more positive choices I could have made in all my situations.

Regarding my most recent situation, I could have sought charitable donations from Mary Jo's Place, a local charity that helps homeless or displaced persons, or I could have sought emergency assistance from the county or sought help from a local church. But I gave none of those options a thought.

And being the man of the house, I should have never allowed my woman's nagging and negativity affect my thoughts and actions. Even in my weakened physical and mental states, I should have stayed spiritually and mentally strong. I did not, as the leader that I am supposed to be, and I am paying the price. Lesson learned.

I have been extremely blessed in all areas of my life, so I have learned to count my blessings rather than question my station in life or the reason behind certain situations. I have faith in my Creator that I can make it through any situation with his help.

Because in the end, all that I've been through is really insignificant. My African American ancestors have been through a collective set of horrific situations at the hands of white folks that are wholly unimaginable to me, situations so horrible and deranged as to boggle the mind. If they could prevail and thrive after such depravity perpetrated against them, then I can prevail in my relatively subtle setbacks. All I have to do is make the choice to do so.

THE END

ABOUT THE AUTHOR

Shane Townsend lives in Minneapolis, Minnesota, with his wife, Kim. Shane is currently employed as a lead material handler and forklift operator at the Resideo building in Golden Valley, Minnesota.

CPSIA information can be obtained
at www.ICGtesting.com
Printed in the USA
LVHW091549050720
659731LV00006B/533